THE ARRANGEMENT 19

The Ferro Family

By:

H.M. Ward

www.SexyAwesomeBooks.com

COPYRIGHT

This book is a work of fiction. Names, characters, places, and incidents are either the product of the author's imagination or are used fictitiously, and any resemblance to actual persons, living or dead, events, or locales is entirely coincidental.

H.M. WARD PRESS
First Edition: June 2015
ISBN: 9781630350758

THE ARRANGEMENT 19

Dear Reader,

The Arrangement Series is different. How? The story is organic—and growing swiftly. Originally intended to be four serial novels, fans of the series demanded more Sean & Avery, spurring an entirely new concept: a fan-driven series. When fans ask for more, I write more.

I am astonished and humbled by the response this series has received. As the series grows, I am constantly fascinated by the requests and insights from readers. This series has sold over 10 MILLION copies! The average length of each book is 125 pages in paperback and can be read in a few hours or less.

This series intertwines with my other work, but is designed to be read independently, as a quick read between other titles.

You can join in the discussion via my Facebook page: www.facebook.com/AuthorHMWard.

For a complete listing of Ferro books, look here: www.SexyAwesomeBooks.com & click BOOKS.

Thank you and happy reading!

~Holly

Chapter 1

Time stops as clouds of smoke drift toward us in slow motion. Ashes flutter through the air, landing on my shoulders like blackened snowflakes. We instinctively throw our helmets to the ground, shedding dead weight for what's to come. My heart pounds in my chest because I know what's going to happen. Sean is going to run back inside. There's no way he's going to leave knowing his mother is still inside the mansion.

Before he has the chance, my feet are moving, gaining traction quickly. My arms swing by my sides, elbows tucked tightly against my ribs, as I summon every last bit of speed I can muster. I move away from Sean, racing toward the side lawn that will wrap around to the room where Constance takes her breakfast. She had to be in that glass room. As the bomb went off, I heard the glass shatter, an explosion of wind chimes hitting cement. There's no way she's alive, but for Sean's sake, I hope she is.

"Avery! Stop!"

Sean's voice rings out behind me, but I can't stop. I don't answer. My feet move, pounding the grass faster and faster. I hit a patch that's too slick. My foot slips to the side and before I can correct it, I hit the ground, tackled from behind. I slide on the damp grass and stop abruptly.

"Stop! Just, stop."

Sean rolls me over, and I want to cry, seeing his beautiful face contorted with fear. Terror seeps into those sexy blue eyes. His dark lashes flutter as he holds me down, pressing my body to the ground beneath him. He sucks in air, trying to catch his breath.

In that moment, I'm aware of little things— the way a bead of sweat rolls off his temple and falls, hitting my skin like a grenade. His breath is warm and perfect, coming in fast puffs as his chest expands against me. His hands are rough, and there's a gash on his palm that covers his fingers in dark red blood. He doesn't seem to notice the wound.

Sean places his hands against my face, holding me still. His lips part as if he wants to speak, but nothing comes out. He's looking at me as if I were his soul and he was about to lose it. His hands slip over my cheeks, shaking before taking a deep breath and pressing his forehead against mine.

"Avery, I can't lose you. Don't—" His voice is too light, too high. The sound cuts off. Sean blinks, and it's easy to see how glassy his eyes have become. My lip quivers as I throw my arms around him.

"I can't lose you either. You can't run inside. Sean, if something happened to you. This is my fault. I—"

But he doesn't let me finish. He lowers his head and presses a soft kiss to my lips. When he pulls away, the trembling has subsided. The steady feel of his hands returns and I know he's taking all the emotion swirling within and banishing it so he can get through this moment. He's in survival mode, and I know he has to do it, but every time he goes back to that place within himself he risks never returning.

I can't fathom a life without emotion, without feeling. No matter how hard I try to disconnect my feelings from my body, I can't. They come rushing to the surface at the worst times.

Like now.

I pull Sean into a tight hug and kiss his face. Sweat clings to his grimy skin as the dust cloud settles over the lawn. I pull back and look at him.

"Promise you'll come back. Promise me." I swallow hard, waiting for a response.

Sean's sapphire eyes lock on mine. Deep within those pure blue orbs, promises mingle with pain. Darkness lies in wait, ready to reclaim him. He can't fight it anymore. It's time to choose between saving Sean from his demons and becoming a monster to save his family. I know his choice.

He pushes off the ground, his expression pure steel, and I can no longer read him. His voice is deep and dangerous. He points toward the other end of the driveway.

"There's a car in the gardener's shed down by the road. I can see it from here. They overlooked it. Take the car to Trystan's and stay with him until I come back." The way he says it is final. There is no other choice. He won't let me go with him. When I don't follow his order to walk away, anger flashes across his eyes. "Avery, I said go!"

Swallowing hard, I fold my arms over my chest and hold his gaze.

"No. I'm staying with you. I won't leave you here, and you're wasting precious time arguing with me."

"You can't be here. If Vic Jr. comes—"

"If he comes, I'll kill him myself." Wow, that sounded scary. When did I become a badass? The tone of my voice makes Sean raise a brow.

"I won't let him hurt you."

"Then don't send me off alone. Sean, come with me." I reach for his hand, but he pulls away.

"I have to get my mother out of there." He watches me for a moment, before grabbing my wrist. "Stay close behind. Do not run in front of me or you'll get a bullet in your ass. Do you understand? I'll shoot you myself if it keeps you from running inside. Do not take off again. Understood?"

As he speaks, my stomach flips and the hairs on the back of my neck stand on end. He means every word.

Chapter 2

I nod once and look back up toward the house. There hasn't been a sound since the last explosion, which is weird. Rescue vehicles should be tearing up the sunrise with noisy sirens, but it's quiet.

Sean leads the way toward the back of the house, stepping over blown-up bits of wall, beams, and what looks like a piece of the front door. The splintered wood is smoldering, sending up a black beam of repugnant smoke. The scent makes me gag as we pass. Sean suddenly pulls his shirt off and rips it in two, then hands one piece to me.

"Tie it on and make sure you cover your nose and mouth, there is too much smoke and ash in the air. If it gets to be too much, tell me and we'll turn back." He looks over his shoulder at me and I know he doesn't want to do this. If we step back into this house, it's possible neither of us will come out.

I do as he says and take the torn piece of fabric and tie it behind my head, adjusting the front to cover my face just below my eyes. Sean turns around, making sure I've done as he wanted. A giggle escapes me when I see his beautiful blue eyes peering over the top of the fabric.

"You're laughing?" He sounds surprised. I shove the smile off my face, but it lights up again. I shrug.

"I'm an emotional lunatic. I can't be held responsible for my giggles. Besides, if I didn't laugh right now, I'd cry instead." Sean rolls his eyes and is about to turn back toward the smoking house when I catch his arm. "Hey. Don't do that to me. You deal with stress your way, and I deal with stress my way. If it helps me to think that we look like we should be robbing a bank and riding off on horses, then let me."

I rise on my tiptoes, in his face and seriously scolding him as I speak. I can't see anything except his eyes, which seem pissed off. It isn't until he laughs that I back down. Sean clears his throat.

"I love you. Be the lunatic you are. Fly your freak flag, Avery. That's one of the reasons why I love you. I'm just worried I'm too late. Mother wasn't supposed to be here." Sean turns back to look at the house. His eyes scan the tree line surrounding the property. His eyes stop and narrow, watching a single spot intently as if he sees something.

I grab his forearm and tug. Sean's eyes glance back at me.

"Thanks, partner." I tip my fake ten-gallon hat toward him. I swear I hear a giggle come from under his mask, and I know he smiles because the corners of his eyes crinkle. I love making him smile.

He takes my hand.

"Let's get inside before another bomb goes off. There was supposed to be one more, according to Masterson. It should have exploded by now."

"Maybe it's a dud?" Can that happen?

"Possibly, but we can't risk it by lingering here. It's possible the bastard rigged the final bomb to explode when the medics show up. It would kill any survivors and ensure Vic's control. Besides," his voice sounds cold and lifeless, the Sean I knew before all this started, "it's what I would do if I had to eliminate an entire family at once."

My stomach twists in response to hearing him admit it. He's no longer the shy Sean that hides behind those dark lashes. That man is long gone, and in his wake is a being more monster than man.

It kills me to hear him talk like this. I need to get us out of this situation and get him away from here. There was a good reason Sean was on the opposite coast, a good reason his stays in New York were short: he was avoiding losing more of himself. Every minute he stays here, another piece of his soul chips away, lost forever. Nothing I can do will change that. Sean would trade his life to save his mother even though she doesn't deserve it.

Part of me expects to walk into the solarium and see her standing in that blood-red robe without a scratch, amongst the rubble, still perfectly pressed and pristine, a teacup in her hand.

If she had anything to do with this, I'm going to strangle her myself.

Sean turns away and heads toward the solarium. We skulk around the property, staying in the gardens that are near the house, but not so close we'll get toasted if another bomb goes off.

The early morning shadows stretch across the lawn, shading us. The dappled light makes us harder to see, but it also masks anyone else who might be out there. I keep scanning the trees, looking for the man who did this— looking for a sibling I never knew existed.

When I was younger, I would have been thrilled to find out I had a brother. I always wanted someone else to play with, but my parents never had another child. To find out that my dad wasn't my father was rough, but finding out my real father was a murderer and my new brother is just as bad—well, it sucks.

I want a refund. I didn't order this life.

This will change me. There's no way to avoid it. I've taken enough classes to know what happens to a person when their past is ripped away and replaced with one they don't want, filled with people they don't want to know. Although I didn't take SO YOUR REAL DAD IS REALLY A MURDERER 101, I know I'll fight an emotional battle I can't win. No matter what, blood is blood. My father was a twisted killer, and my brother is just as bad.

We step into a clearing, and the sight of the once grand solarium jerks me from my thoughts. It's cracked open like an egg with smoke billowing out the remains of the roof. Twisted metal hangs from the top of the dome, dangling pieces of broken glass still clinging desperately to the frame. Every few seconds the deathly silence breaks with sounds of fire crackling, glass breaking, metal clattering. In between those sounds is nothing but silence.

Sean doesn't stop at the twisted threshold. Instead, he ducks through the bent, blackened metal and walks inside.

"Mother! Where are you?" He calls out, but there's no answer.

My heart pounds in my ears as Sean releases my hand. He steps forward, crunching glass beneath his feet. He lifts burnt palm fronds and large pieces of shattered pots, digging a path to the other side of the room. The part of the solarium attached to the house still stands, glass roof intact. If he can get to it, he can see the spot where his mother habitually takes her breakfast each morning.

I keep thinking about what he said. She wasn't supposed to be here.

Images flash through my mind of a younger Constance raising three little boys. I wonder if Sean played out here as a child. I wonder if, as he steps down and hears glass break beneath his feet, a childhood memory shatters with each step.

I glance around the room and try not to choke. Ashes are floating through the air, making it difficult to see. I walk carefully, looking around as I do so, hoping for any sign of his mother. Sean continues to clear a path toward the bistro table on the other side of the room. I linger behind him, scanning the debris for signs of life.

"Constance? Are you in here?" I call out, hoping for an answer, but no one replies.

Sean bends over and lifts a beam that was once part of the rafter. The muscles in his neck are corded tight as he tries to move it. He looks over at me and pulls down his mask.

"I can't get through."

"Sean, she's not here." I don't want to say it, but there's no indication that Constance was out here, other than the noises on the phone. "Maybe she was inside?"

Maybe she was the one who did this. I think it, but I can't say it. Not yet.

"No, her voice," he says, shaking his head. "She was here. The glass and the way the sound came through the headset. She had to be in this room. There was too much glass."

He closes his eyes for a second, then tips his head back and looks up at the sky, before wiping the sweat off his face. His chest is glistening with a thin sheen of sweat. It's insanely hot in here. There are small fires burning all around us, mostly in little piles where

I assume Constance's plants caught fire. Sean puts his hands on his trim hips and looks over at me. His stomach is ripped, tense, and ready to do whatever needed. I manage to make my way over to him and put a hand on his arm.

"Sean, she's not here."

"She has to be. She wouldn't have…" Sean shakes his head as his words die in his mouth. He works his jaw and looks like he's about to scream when we both hear a faint sound. We twist toward the noise and then look back at each other.

"Did you hear that?"

Sean nods and puts a finger to his lips. He waits, and we hear it again. It sounds like someone is crying, softly, weakly. Sean crouches and peers through the debris. I copy him and scan the room. That's when I see it—a broken teacup in the rubble. The handle is missing, but the base is intact. I stiffen when my eyes notice the other part.

"Sean." I grip his bare arm and crouch toward it. "That's? Is it?"

Sean is still. I don't know if he doesn't see it or can't believe what he's seeing. A few feet in front of us, hidden between shards of pottery and under a fallen pane of glass, is the handle of the cup, a single finger wrapped around it. The finger is thin and feminine, its nail polished blood red.

I gasp and stare, as my stomach twists, threatening to spew any contents on the floor. This isn't happening. It can't be. Trembling, I scan the room for the rest of the body. Sean still hasn't moved; his eyes lock on a spot to my left, not far from the first piece of the teacup. Under a massive metal beam, once belonging high in the rafters and now resting uselessly on the floor, is a pale arm. Blood covers the palm, pooling in the center like a liquid gemstone.

"Mom." He says the word like he's conjuring a ghost and rushes toward her. Sean touches his mother's arm, telling her she'll be all right, as I watch in horror.

Constance's body is under that beam. The only parts sticking out are her forearm and wrist. Sean tries to push the beam off of her, but it doesn't move. He tries again and again to get it to budge, but there's no way it will budge without a crane.

He tells her again, "I'll get you out. You'll be all right." Sean pushes his shoulder to the metal and tries to lift it again. He grits his teeth and veins pop up all over his neck and chest as he does it. The beam begins to shift. Snapping out of my shock, I drop to my knees and take her limp hand.

"Constance! I'll pull you out! Hold on!"

Sean's face is dripping with sweat. His body is strained and shaking as he tries to lift the beam higher, but he does it. Every muscle in his body quivers as he manages to lift it off the ground.

I don't hesitate. I take hold of Constance's wrist and pull. The opening is small, but it provides enough to get her out.

Sean screams in pain as he tries to hold the beam up for another second. I pull on her arm expecting her to shift, but she doesn't. The beam must be on her shoulder or something because it takes a lot more force to get her to move. Tears prick my eyes, and I try to blink them away, but it just clouds my vision.

Sean's yell makes me try harder. I dig in my heels and lean back, giving it everything. Broken shoulder or not, there's no way she should be this stuck. When the beam lifts that final bit, her arm breaks free. I fall back expecting to see a rumpled Constance Ferro on the floor in front of me, her face bloodied, her gown torn. I expect broken bones and a face that will need stitches.

But it's not what I expected to see at all.

Sean drops the rafter and falls to the ground, shaking with anger and tears flooding from his eyes, and screams. The sound rips my soul in two.

On the floor, in the debris, is a severed arm with a gold ring still on one of her fingers. The pattern is unmistakable—it's the Ferro family crest.

It's his mother's ring. The one she wears every day and never takes off.

Constance Ferro is dead.

Chapter 3

My throat tightens as I hear Sean cry out. I know he didn't get along with his mother, hell she hated him—she hated everyone—so the extent of his reaction surprises me a little bit. I had no idea how much he cared for her despite her evilness.

I don't know what to think about this, about any of it. I stare at the severed arm and wish to God this never happened. The position of her arm makes it look as if she were asleep. Swallowing hard, I try not to choke. I'm so close to totally losing it, but I can't because of Sean.

If I saw my mother blown apart, I'd lose it. I'd scream until my lungs burned, and my throat was raw. Terror would creep up my spine like an icy finger and make me sick. I'd see the world around me freeze. The flurry of meaningless daily tasks would blast from my mind. Every worry, every thought would be blown away—except for thoughts of her.

Regret for all the things I didn't get to say or do would consume me. I'd wonder if she was in pain when she died. The thoughts have no words at first. They fall slowly, becoming clearer as they land, little pieces of ash drifting through the air.

Sean is living in that nightmare, the worst thought playing across his face—he failed to save her. He came close, but his failure means Constance's death.

Throat tight and burning, I pad over the glass-covered floor and kneel next to Sean. I raise my hand to place it on his shoulder, my palm hovering over him, unsure of what to do. I want to pull him out of that thought. He couldn't have saved her. He couldn't have saved Amanda. I wrestle with the same thought of saving my parents. I feel the guilt of it around my neck squeezing the life out of me.

Sometimes there is no fault, no blame. Even if there is a finger to point at someone, it's not Sean. The man lives a double life. There's a hardened exterior that's cruel and frightening, but beneath the surface is a broken man with too much empathy to live with loss. The explosion adds one more life to the pile, one more person to mourn, and one more person to twist his tortured soul until he falls apart.

"Sean."

He doesn't move. His chest expands as he breathes and chokes back an angry sob. Those dark eyes focus on his mother's ring; his lower lids twitch upward as if he can't control them any longer. His jaw locks and he shakes his head.

Shock is a strange thing. At first it felt like I could pull us both to safety. I thought we'd save his mother and run out of here, but the queasy feeling in my stomach won't let up. The only thing I can think about is his mother sitting out here, pressing the phone to her ear, scolding Sean right before the room exploded. Did she know she was going to die? She had to know, she screamed horrifically over the phone. It's not a sound easily forgotten.

I try to swallow, but can't. The lump in my throat won't move. My legs buckle, and I hug my knees tighter, intending to bury my face.

Sean's voice makes me tip `my head to the side.

"Avery?"

I blink once, slowly. Suddenly, the room shifts violently and my face lands hard against shards of glass on the floor. I try to shake it off and sit up, but I can't. The room won't stop spinning. I blink a few times, trying to focus my eyes and failing. Sean's voice echoes as if he were far away.

Constance's ring is the last thing I see before the world goes dark.

Chapter 4

My body prickles with goose bumps, but I can't feel the night air. I move my hand through the thin layer of fog feeling nothing.

I'm not outside. I'm alone, standing in the middle of a vacant room. There are no walls, only darkness. I don't know where I am. My heart thumps harder in my chest, and I can't breathe. There's smoke. It's everywhere, filling the room from top to bottom in thick, billowy black clouds.

I scream out for Sean, but I have no voice. I try again, but the only sound is a blood-curdling scream. It seems like it will never end. I fall to my knees and press my face to the floor, covering my head. Tears streak my cheeks, but I can't feel them. I don't feel the heat of the room or the smoke, but it chokes me all the same.

My body betrays me, and I slump to the floor like a rag doll, no longer able to move. It's like I'm trapped on tar paper, pinned in place. I open my mouth and inhale deeply, intending to scream as loud as I can, but the scream is silent.

No one can hear me. I'll die here, alone.

I blink, trying to focus. Across from me, like a tiny sun in the darkness, something flashed. I blink away the smoke and swallow the pain, trying to see what it is. I reach out toward the light and find a familiar touch—Sean. He's wearing his mother's ring on his pinky. He reaches out toward me and takes my hand.

"I'm sorry, Avery." His words are a whisper. They carry through the smoke and touch my ears like a kiss.

Fear courses through my veins. Is he giving up? We can't die here! Sean's grip on my hand loosens, so I tighten my fist. I try to yell,

"NO! Don't leave me! Sean!"

I manage to pull my heavy body forward, enough to grip his hand firmly. I want to pull his hand to my cheek. I want to touch him, to hold him one last time.

My stomach is in knots as fear pushes my pulse into the stroke zone. I say things, things that have no meaning and lift his heavy hand, pulling it toward me. I press the back of his palm to my cheek, and when I lower my mouth to his skin, I press my lips to his skin.

When I open my eyes, I see what I'm holding—Sean's severed arm, dripping with blood. A scream rakes through my body, bellowing out of my mouth.

I shoot up, covered in sweat and wailing like a banshee.

A hand firmly grabs me and silences my shriek. Sean's warm breath brushes against my ear.

"You're all right. Avery, we need to be quiet. Vic's men are still here."

I blink, confused. Slowly, I turn toward Sean, heart still pounding in my chest.

"You're alive." Tears sting my eyes as I throw my arms around his neck. "Oh, God, Sean."

"You were dreaming. I'm right here," he says, kissing the top of my head.

He holds me for a moment; his touch normally chases away my nightmares, but this time it doesn't. Those hands, those strong, sure hands will end up as lifeless as his mother's hands. A lump the size of a tennis ball forms in my throat. I can't imagine my world without him.

This is my fault. All of it.

Sean pulls back but holds onto my shoulders. He offers a small smile before pushing a lock of hair out of my eyes.

"You've been through Hell today. If you didn't have nightmares, I'd be worried. It's okay, Avery."

My lips try to pull into a smile, but they quiver and fall. I'm going to lose him. If we keep going down this path, Sean will end up beneath six feet of dirt. I look away, not wanting him to see my thoughts.

My brows pull together as I notice my surroundings. Planks of age-darkened wood cover the walls and floor. A patch of moonlight shines through the roof, casting silver light across the aged floor. In the center of the small room is the trunk of a massive oak tree. I blink again.

"How hard did I hit my head?"

Translation: Where the fuck are we?

"Welcome to Casa Dei Diamanti," Sean answers, laughing. He breathes in the night air lustily, mirth reaching his eyes for a brief moment before the sadness sucks it away again.

"Welcome to the demented house? Seriously?" My eyebrow shoots up inquisitively.

Sean shakes his head, his dark locks falling forward. When he looks up, he glances up at me from beneath those dark lashes, as if he were going to share some deep dark secret.

"You're joking, right? Everyone has to take a second language in high school. You are an over-educated woman, Miss College Graduate. How do you not know what 'diamanti' means?"

Offended, I smile with feigned patience.

"Spill, Mr. Jones. Where am I? The Batcave? Did the tree lift your evil underground lair into the sky as it grew?"

He snort-laughs boyishly as if I tickled him in the perfect spot.

"Why does everyone say that? I wasn't a dark child." He drops his gaze and looks at his hands, his tone serious now. "That came later, much later."

I know this place is right on top of a raw nerve for him, but I'm not sure why. I look around, hoping he'll tell me more, but he's silent. There's a chest on the side of the room, right below a little window. There's no sign of the escape hatch or hole in the floor, but there is a rickety rope ladder piled into the corner. I wonder how he got me up here. He must have carried me.

The ceiling is low and crumbling, cedar shakes tumbling through holes in the roof. In its heyday, the little fort must have been swicked. I feel almost sad to see it in such disrepair, vines and branches growing through it unchecked.

"So, we're still by the mansion, then?" I ask, crawling over to the window. I test the floor carefully, pressing on each plank, worried I'll fall through.

"It's sturdy. You won't fall. And yes, we're still by the house." Sean scoots back and leans against the wall.

I glance over the sill and look out. All I can see is trees. Disappointed, I sit back down. The floor beneath me creaks under my weight, and I crab-crawl forward toward the tree.

"Are you sure this isn't like Owl's house? That sucker blew away with Piglet and Pooh in it."

"Are you talking about a children's book?" Sean blinks and grins.

"Winnie the Pooh was stuffed with fluff. I'm a little more, well, stuffed with bones that don't want to shatter when this thing falls out of the sky."

My heart is racing, unable to calm down. Sean smiles softly, taking my hand and pulling me toward him. I shake my head, refusing to move.

"Are you afraid of heights, Miss Smith?"

"Only when there isn't a plane around me."

"Seriously?" Amusement lights his face, his expression betraying his belief that this is a silly thing to fear.

"Tell me something," I say nodding and closing my eyes tightly. "Talk, or I'm going to flip out."

He notices the way I'm shaking and comes to sit beside me. He places his hand on top of mine and gently squeezes it.

"We're in my old tree house. Peter and I played up here as children. I had a tendency to find the tallest tree and climb it. My mother," his voice catches in his throat, but he spits out the rest of the thought, "didn't like it, but my father encouraged us to climb higher and go further. One day he took us back here and asked which tree I liked best. I picked this one. I showed him how high I could climb. The next time he walked us out this way, this tree house was two limbs higher than I'd climbed. When we were children, the man was always pushing us to go further, to climb higher, and to dream bigger. God, he's changed." Sean rubs his hand over his face and tips his head back against the wall.

"So, once upon a time, your dad was nice?"

Sean's eyes cut over to me. He shrugs.

"Yeah, he was. Before the mistresses came around, he gave Pete and me all his attention.

He told me that I could have this place and do anything I wanted with it if I could get up here. There wasn't a ladder. It took me a month to get up here. I suppose it was more for me than Pete. He was still young then and couldn't climb the way I did. Dad added the ladder later for him."

"So, you played up here when you were little?" I look around again, wondering about the man sitting next to me. It's a normal tree house, except that it's practically in the clouds.

"Yeah, I did. I can't remember the last time I was up here. I had to be thirteen or so." He smiles softly, lost in thought. "I'd just had my first kiss, and came up here afterward to get away from Pete and Jon. By then, it was overgrown and aging poorly. This morning, I almost couldn't find it. The forest has grown up around it, devouring it."

The terror melts away as he speaks, and I get to see a side that he usually keeps hidden.

"First kiss?"

"Yeah." He smiles. "It was sweet and quick. But at the time, it felt like a lifetime of bliss." Sean realizes he has a smile on his face, and it vanishes.

"Sean Ferro kissed a girl sweetly? I can't imagine it. That's like saying Dracula's teeth are candy corn."

"How is that the same?" His eyes are laughing as he looks at me, and all I want is to keep him looking just like this.

"Well, you think that he's going to be all mean and nasty, but no—alas! The dark dude in the cape with a taste for blood is just a sugar addict who—"

"You did not just compare me to Dracula," Sean interrupts.

"Blah! I vant to suck your sveets!" I hold up my hands and point my fingers down like teeth, speaking with my best Transylvanian accent. Sean's eyes go wide, and then he actually giggles.

"You're insane."

"Holy shit! You giggled. I heard it." I grab his ultra tight shirt and yank him toward me. "Open." I tap his lips. "I need to check your teeth."

Sean watches my mouth as I speak, with the sweet grin still in place. It's so unlike him that it makes my stomach flip. He reaches for me slowly and, when our eyes meet, he holds my gaze. Sean brushes his hand against my cheek and slides his fingers around the back of my neck. His other hand finds my cheek and inch-by-inch he gets closer. My pulse is hammering in my ears, and it's all I can do to not squeal. Butterflies erupt in my stomach and move through me in waves. The fierce flutter makes it hard to breathe as Sean's beautiful mouth gets closer.

Normally he takes what he wants or tells me to, but this is different. It has me supercharged, and every inch of me is tingling. It's like I licked an electrical socket. I can't move. I want to lean into the kiss, but I want to see what he's going to do. The way he moves toward me and looks at me through those dark lashes, the way he cradles my head and cups my cheek—it's as if he's asking and it leaves me trembling.

He stops right before our lips touch, a breath away. His gaze drops to my mouth, and he pauses, not kissing, just waiting. I can't move. The magic of the moment makes the rest of the world melt away. It feels pure and perfect. I didn't know he could be like this.

Sean reveals another version of him, one long buried. I'm drawn to him, pulled to his mouth. I want his arms to hold me tight, but there's nothing harsh or hurried. His breath washes over my mouth, and my lips part slightly, wanting him, waiting for him to kiss me.

Sean's dark lashes flutter closed, and he leans in, gently brushing his lips against mine. The butterflies wiz through me as his touch sets off a shower of sparks. The smoothness of his bottom lip against mine, the way he moves surely and gently sets every inch of me on fire. I want more, but he doesn't deepen the kiss. Instead, he slowly slides his lips closed before pressing them to mine, and then pulls away.

I'm breathless. The kiss feels like it froze time, but it passes too quickly. It's an enigma I don't understand. I blink wildly, and try to fathom why that affected me so much.

Sean doesn't smile or say any of the assy things he usually does. He doesn't try to own me, make me, or command me. He just pulls away, as if he didn't know what he did to me. How can one kiss do that?

After a moment, I manage to catch his eye. The corner of his mouth pulls up, and he quickly looks away. My chest tightens as my heart beats harder. My impulse is telling me to jump him, but there's something so fragile about him that I can't.

My chest rises and falls, as I suck in way too much air. I can't hide what that did to me, how it made me feel. I finally breathe his name.

"Sean?" He glances at me from the corner of his eye.

"Yeah?"

What do I say? I want to ask him why he doesn't love me like that, but how can I? He mentions his first kiss and sugar, then gives me this orgasmically mind-blowing kiss. What the fuck? I can't say any of it though, so I just sit there gaping, my mouth hanging open. He smirks.

"So I suppose you like sweet kisses, now?"

"I like your kisses, all of them. I like how you surprise me, how there's always another side of you that I haven't seen before. You literally took my breath away. Do you know how rare that is?" I stare at him and think that he honestly doesn't know.

"It's not something I like to do." He looks down at his hands, and I swear he's sitting like a teenager, shoulders slumped forward, his back curved, and lowers his head into his hands. "It's too—" He sucks in a shaky breath and finishes, "invasive."

That's not the word I thought he was going to say.

"How so?"

"It reveals something about you, about me," he says without looking at me. "It's vulnerability and weakness wrapped in pleasure. Pleasure has a way of stripping everything else away and making decisions we normally wouldn't make. I swore I'd never kiss someone like that again."

I don't know what to say. It feels like he just told me a big secret—I can feel the weight of it—but I can't see how he got there. I touch his knee.

"We can't change who we are, Sean. Kisses like that are rare. It lasted forever, but not long enough. Sean, I've had sweet kisses before. That's not it. It's not that I'm a candy fang banger, either." He smiles and looks over at me. "It's you. It's when you let yourself be seen— that's the difference."

His lips part like he wants to say something, but he closes his eyes and looks away. Tipping his head against the wall, he opens those dark eyes and looks at the starry sky.

"I have trouble with that. I know that's an understatement, but it's hard to give someone a piece of your heart willingly only to have it torn away. A person can only do that so many times."

"Yeah, but you still have a heart to give." I bump his knees with mine. "Even after everything you've experienced. Sean, you're not normal, and I think that's great." I smile at him.

He swallows hard and looks over at me. "Another piece of me died today. When saw my mother's hand on the teacup, I thought she was dead. Then we found her. Avery, I thought we could pull her out. I thought... I wanted her to be somehow still alive."

I press my lips together and drape my arm over his shoulder.

"So did I."

"I know you did." Sean smiles weakly at me and takes a deep breath. His chest fills and slowly rises before he lets it out. "I keep making the mistake of thinking everything will work out, that I have time to fix my mistakes."

"She can still hear you. I'm pretty sure you know that, otherwise I wouldn't have seen you talking to a headstone. Unless crazy is contagious because I do it all the time." I smile at him for a brief moment. "It's never too late." He looks over at me, surprised.

"And you really believe this?"

"Yeah, I do." I nod, secretly shocked by my sudden certainty. "I guess that's why I didn't get sucked down an emotional black hole when they died, or with any of the shit that happened after. No matter what, I'm not totally alone. They hear me, even if I can't hear them anymore. If I did, I think I'd pee myself." I laugh and squirm thinking about it.

"Thank you for not questioning me about my mother or our relationship. You took it as a given that she loved me and that I returned the affection in my way."

I do believe he loved her, but I'm not as sure about Constance. I study the old boards and wonder about the younger version of the Ice Queen, the version who worried her son would fall from a tree. I wonder how she turned into the cold, conniving woman who sat in the solarium each morning, the woman who wanted me gone.

I don't want people to wonder about me. I don't want to go down that road.

"Hey," I say to Sean, bumping his shoulder with mine. When he looks over at me with those blue eyes, I say, "Promise me something."

"Anything."

"Promise me that we'll have one more sweet kiss. Not right now, but at some time when things are normal and ninjas aren't hunting us down." I look toward the window, glad no one tended to this part of the woods. If they had, there'd be nowhere to hide.

"They aren't ninjas or we'd be dead already. Our saving grace is that Vic cheaply surrounded himself with bargain basement thugs instead of trained assassins." He turns and boops my nose. "Miss Smith, I think you might be a candy fang banger after all, but I'll grant your request. Reserved for you is one completely vulnerable kiss with no walls up, no distance, and no hidden heart. Just promise me you'll use it for good and not evil."

I smile so hard my face hurts.

"You know I'm going to refer to this place from now on as the Batcave, right?"

"It's because you want to say,"

We say it together, and laugh, "To the Batcave!"

Chapter 5

My eyes flutter open, and I blink the sleep from my eyes. It takes me a moment to remember where I am. There's a wooden board beneath my head and an arm draped over my waist; I smile as I realize it's Sean.

I roll towards him and my stomach rumbles. He looks like he hasn't slept in days. There are dark circles under his eyes. He's awake and watching me.

"Good morning, beautiful."

I smile at him, taking in his messy hair, scruffy face, and a tiny t-shirt. I look at it again, finally realizing what it is. Across the chest of the rust colored shirt, written in a burnt coffee color are the words CROSS COUNTRY. The rest is too faded to read.

"Was this yours?"

"A million years ago," he says nodding.

"You were a runner?"

Sean sits up and stretches, the tiny shirt revealing his hard stomach as he moves. He leans back against the wall and tugs the hem down.

"Yeah, it was one of the few school activities I enjoyed. Our father shoved us into everything else. God, you should have seen his face when Peter started swing dancing. The saddle shoes made the old man think Pete changed teams." Sean laughs once remembering something from long ago.

"I've never heard you say much about your dad." I tread carefully. Sean's a raw mess of emotions, which means he's trying to keep everything locked up, but he'll erupt at some point and go ape-shit crazy. "But I like the tight shirt; it's sexy."

He grins and looks down at the shirt before running his hands over the faded text.

"Dad was difficult." He pauses, searching for the right words. "He was either there too much or completely gone. He always went to extremes."

I smile faintly before my stomach rumbles again, louder this time. Sean looks over at me.

"I'm sorry, we can't grab pancakes. I wish things were different." He crawls across the tree house floor and opens the old chest, pulling out bottled water and a silver wrapper that looks like a candy bar. He tosses them to me.

"You stocked the tree house?"

"Not me, Jon," he says, shaking his head. "He was a little paranoid a while back. Those meal bars last a decade. The water is a little questionable, but I drank it, and I'm still here. You'll be fine."

I rip the wrapper open and stuff the meal bar in my mouth. I'm starving. It doesn't matter that it tastes like a combo of hay, clay, and bark.

"So, what's with you and Jon?" He looks over at me.

"What do you mean?"

"It seems like there's some tension there. I mean, not from you—you come across tense with everyone—but from Jon. He's easy going with everyone except with you. Did you guys have a fight or something?"

Sean takes a slow pull of air and lets it out, then runs his hands through his hair.

"Something."

Okay. I guess we aren't talking about that.

Sean gets up and looks down. The sun isn't quite up yet and the morning sky is light blue with a spattering of stars just barely visible through the treetops. He looks back at me.

"Time to meet up with Masterson."

"Yeah. Marty." I don't know what to think of him anymore. I don't like that he got so close to me, without my having any idea who he really is. It freaks me out. I glance at Sean wondering how much I still don't know about him.

"He's an asset this way, and his being enamored with you has kept you alive. Come on." He tosses the ladder over the side.

I go to throw my leg over the side and look down. My heart jumps up my throat and falls out the window. "Holy shit! We're up high!"

"You looked last night," he points out, laughing.

"It was pitch black last night. The ground is much further away than I thought. Who the hell puts a kid's tree house thirty feet in the air?"

"My father. And we're not that high. You can do it. Just go one step at a time and don't look down."

"Fuckbunnies." I mutter the word under my breath and toss my leg over the sill. My foot finds the first rung, and I slide the rest of my body over the edge and down the ladder. The muttering doesn't stop until my feet hit the grass. "Thank God!"

Sean jumps down behind me, skipping the last few rungs. He slips his hands around my waist and pulls me close.

"I didn't think you were a religious person."

"I'm not, not really. Why?"

"You were praying the entire way down. I would have thought you'd be cursing up a storm, and you're reciting Psalms. How do you even know them?" Sean looks surprised. I shrug.

"My mom used to say stuff. I never really thought about it."

"Come on." He takes my hand and we head toward the shed at the edge of the property. We shove through a door into a dark space that smells like grass seed and chemicals before seeing a lump of canvas covering a car. It's hidden behind a ton of lawn equipment.

Sean rushes toward it and pulls off the cover. I blink at it several times before saying, "Holy shit! It's the Batmobile!" There's a pimped out matte black Maserati, with a shiny black racing stripe down the center. It's got black rims and black glass. The thing looks totally swicked. "Why do you have this? Is there something you're not telling me?"

Sean ignores me and grabs a key from under the front wheel well and unlocks the door.

"Get in." I jump inside and yank my door closed.

"So, are you going to tell me?" Sean starts the engine and the thing purrs to life. It looks new. I lean over and look at the odometer. It is new! I slip my fingers over the Italian leather and moan. "Is this the gardener's car? Because if it is, I picked the wrong major by a long shot. I should have studied horticulture, 'cuz damn!"

Sean's lips tug up in the corner. He presses a button, and a garage door lifts behind us. Sean backs up carefully, then shifts into drive, the car rumbling sensually beneath us.

"It was Jon's. Remember how he was acting like an irresponsible asshole?" I nod. "I took his car away and hid it in the shed." I blink at him as he steers down the gravel path.

"You hid a million dollar car in the shed?"

"Yeah, I was trying to teach him a lesson." Sean is straight-faced when he says it, but there's a tiny twitch in the corner of his mouth like he wants to smile. I run my hands over the dashboard's sexy curves before sitting back into my seat.

"Did it work?"

"Hell if I know. He went out and bought a cheaper car. The asshat thought he lost this one. He didn't even tell our mother it was gone."

Sean navigates through the back of the property until we intersect with one of the back roads. He floors it, and the car roars to life. It's the coolest car sound ever.

"Let me get this straight: Jon thinks he misplaced an entire car?" Sean nods and jerks the wheel as we speed away from the mansion, passing by a line of emergency vehicles as we do so. "So, you can lose a million bucks and not feel it?"

Sean steals a glance at me from the corner of his eye. He's driving a sick car, shirtless, and covered in sweat. The slight twitch of his lips makes him nearly irresistible.

"Maybe."

"Maybe means yes." I grin and settle back into the seat. "So, a million bucks is like a penny to you? If you saw it on the sidewalk, you'd just keep walking? Wow." I'm silent for a moment, thinking. I twist my palms together and look away from him, out the window.

"I didn't say that, you did, and I know that look. Whatever you're thinking, it's wrong." Sean is taking back roads and racing insanely fast towards the beach. I glance over at him.

"I did a lot more for a lot less. That doesn't bother you?" I watch him for a moment, wondering what he must think of me. I lower my lashes and stare at my hands in my lap. Sean reaches over and takes my hand.

"You are worth more than anything I own, anything I have. I'm glad you didn't let me send you away that first night. I'm glad you left the room and played the piano with me. Avery, I'd give up everything for you. A woman like you comes along once a century, and you're mine."

I look at the gashes on the back of his hand and mentally list everything he lost because of me. If I hadn't entered his life, his mother would be alive, and his home would be more than ashes, smoke, and rubble. I can't say what needs to happen, but I already know. I offer a weak smile and squeeze his hand gently.

"I love you, Sean."

"I love you, too. We'll get through this, Avery."

Chapter 6

We drive on in silence, each of us lost in our thoughts until we come to the causeway that leads to Oak Island. It's a wide-open road surrounded by sand dunes and beach grass. There are scattered deer among the low trees, feeding along the road. Sean floors it, and we fly over the first bridge so fast that my stomach is in my spine.

I shriek and look for the 'oh shit' strap, but there isn't one. Sean grins and glances over at me.

"You like that?"

Before I can say no, he floors it, and we dart away even faster. My knees are coming up, and I'm ready to curl into a ball and scream my head off. But Sean slows down before it gets that bad.

"What's with you?" He sounds perplexed. I want to slap him. I can barely breathe.

"I hate bridges and you were driving 200 miles per hour over one!"

"You're afraid of bridges? Is it because of trolls?"

A hysterical high-pitched laugh escapes my throat, and I look over at him.

"Trolls?"

"I thought you'd have a colorful answer. Sorry. Didn't mean to make you freak out. Well, not that much." He winks at me, then pulls into a parking lot. He rolls to a stop and grins. "Perfect."

Sean drives the car up next to a group of kids. They can't be more than sixteen and, from the looks of it, they're really bored. They all watch as we get out of the car. A kid with a beanie on his shaggy hair stands up. He might be a little stoned.

"Gnarly ride, man. Is that, like, a real Maz?"

Okay, he's super stoned. Another guy with a skateboard stands up and hands his friend a log of cured meat. It looks like a Christmas sausage from Hickory Farms. The stoner bites off a piece and chews it like a goat.

"Yeah, it is." Sean nods and tosses the keys at the kid.

It makes the guy drop his meat log and cover his face. He screams as he does it while his friend laughs like it was the funniest thing ever. The keys peg him in the head and fall to the ground.

"What the hell, dude?" He drops his hands from his face, glaring at Sean.

"Do you like the car?" Sean is too Sean-ish to deal with them. His tone is beyond exasperated.

"Fuck yeah." Both guys reply in unison.

"I'll let you take it for a drive if you agree to do me one little favor." Sean looks at the four kids, scanning their eyes for signs of coherency. The chick sitting on the curb doesn't look up, but I can tell she's having a WTF moment. The guys are too pumped to notice how weird this is.

"Sure, man. Whatever you want."

"Good. Take the car some place with no cameras, beat the shit out of it, and leave it there. No cops and you can't get caught." Sean points at the girl on the curb. "I strongly suggest that girl drives, since she's the only one of you that's still sober."

Everyone in the little group turns and looks at the girl. She has long blue hair tucked beneath a black barrette. She's suddenly staring at her feet so intently her gaze could burn holes straight through them. Sean's right, she's not stoned, just pretending to be.

"Why would you think—" Sean cuts her off.

"Seriously? Are you going to let one of them drive? You'll end up falling off the bridge. I'd find that an unpleasant experience." She looks up and smiles.

"Hey, don't I know you?"

"It's unlikely." Sean's voice is flat.

The girl's gaze drifts over Sean's abs peeking through the bottom of his tiny tee and then over to me. She frowns and looks at the car.

"Why do you want to wreck it? It's a sweet ride." Sean sighs and pulls a lump of cash out of his pocket.

"No questions. Take this and buy a station wagon or something. It's win-win--your friends will follow you around because you have the wheels, you won't have to smoke that shit, and they won't care." He holds out a wad of hundred dollar bills that could easily be three grand. The girl isn't stupid though. She looks over at me, and I wonder if this is a good idea.

"What if they get caught?" He looks at me like I have bricks in my brain.

"Then Jon says he lent it to them. Since he can't remember where he put the damn thing, he won't say it was stolen." He turns back to the chick. "But it's better if you don't get caught."

"So why trash it then?" I ask even though I shouldn't.

"So Jon can't get into more trouble when he finds it." Sean looks back at the girl. "Do we have a deal?"

She takes the money and smiles, before bending down to pick up the fallen keys. The guys she's with pump their fists and holler, "Shotgun!"

They slip inside, and she starts the engine. As she revs the engine, they roll the windows down, and I can hear them yelling as she speeds away, "To the Batcave!"

"I don't want them to get in trouble," I say, looking over at Sean.

"As long as they don't knock over a liquor store, I think they'll be fine. No one is looking for the car, except Jon, and honestly it's possible that he's forgotten. It's been a while since I took it." I smile and fall into step with him.

"I can't believe you did that."

"I can't believe Jon never goes in the shed."

We both smile a little and start walking toward the water. We need to walk down a few dunes to get to the boat. It's better to do it in a spot where there are other people. Most of the male runners around us shuck their shirts, so

Sean blends in a bit more if we're walking among them. As we pass a trashcan, he pulls off his shirt and tosses it in. I've got my bare-chested man back.

As the sun creeps higher in the sky, the morning light paints the clouds orange and pink. I breathe in deeply, enjoying the sea spray and the wind in my hair as I walk hand in hand with Sean. I wish I could freeze time and keep things like this, locked in this moment when it's just him and me, neither of us consumed by grief or heartache.

That thought solidifies something, a nagging sensation that didn't materialize until now. It's clear—there's only one path that leads to Sean's happiness, and this isn't it.

·Chapter 7

When we arrive at Marty's house, it's empty. Sean and I both stuff our faces with leftovers from the refrigerator and then head for the couch. Sean sits down and pats the seat next to him. I stare at his hand, at the way he touches the seat, and think about his mother's lifeless arm, her body blown to pieces. It could have been Sean. The only reason he's still alive right now is because of Marty. Sean wouldn't have been in the mansion if it weren't for me. I'm going to get him killed. Sean glances up at me with those beautiful blue eyes.

"Stop thinking so much." Smirking, I sit down and tuck my leg under my butt, before leaning into him.

"Easy to say, not so easy to do."

We sit there in silence, and before I know what happens, I'm in the black room again. The smoke forms little black clouds that engulf me whole. I can't see. I'm stuck, and then I hear his voice. It sounds like he's far away, but I see his hand—I see that ring flashing in front of my eyes. I reach out and take it.

Gripping Sean's arm, I try to pull him to safety, but there is nowhere safe. I'm holding a severed hand, still dripping with blood. A scream rips through me, and I'm awake.

Sitting up, I gasp and look around. Sean isn't next to me anymore.

"Oh, God."

I throw my legs on the floor and rub my face. I stay like that for a moment, willing my heart to slow, when I hear the creak of wood floorboards. It could be a floorboard on the back porch. My spine goes straight, and my eyes widen. I get up and rush over to the wall, careful not to make a sound.

I don't see Sean, just Marty's granny furniture. I slide along the wall until I'm in a tiny kitchen. The back door is open, swinging gently in the wind, its window curtain flapping. The sound comes a second time. It's closer, louder.

I can't see anyone. It has to be Sean, but the way my body reacts makes me think it isn't. As I inch closer to the window that overlooks the porch, I hold my breath. As I inch up to peer out the window, a voice booms behind me.

"What the hell are you doing?" Marty laughs and steps toward me. I scream like someone stuck a fork in my eye and fall on my ass.

"Marty? When did you get here?"

"Uh, last night. You slept for nearly twenty-four hours straight, princess."

Confused, I look out the window. It's sunrise. Did I seriously sleep that long?

"Really?"

"Yeah, but don't worry about it. You were run ragged. You could probably sleep for a week."

As Marty talks, I look him over. He's more tan than usual, and he's wearing tight black jeans and a fitted pocket t-shirt. His sandy hair is getting longer, so he's slicked it back. He would look kinda nice if he weren't a freaking hit-man.

"Don't give me that look." He scolds, wagging a finger at me before sitting on a counter top.

"Like what? Like you lie too much or like I slept next to you, poured my heart out, and have no idea who you really are? 'Cuz they both suck." Marty rolls his eyes. He slides off the counter.

"Go chew some Midol, princess. We can't all be as forthright as you are. Oh wait, that's right—you lie like a dog, too. Not to mention that you're rather smelly. If you don't mind, shower, then we can fight."

"I hate you." I say the words without feeling, not meaning them. It's more like I hate the fact that I still like him, that I still care about him.

He walks into a hallway, plucks a towel from a closet and hurls it at my head.

"Yeah, yeah. Tell me something I don't know. I put fresh clothes in the bathroom for you."

Tucking the towel under my arm, I shove past him. Marty stops me with his arm and looks down at me. His hair falls forward, softening his features.

"I'm glad you're safe."

I look up at him and want to cry. I want to tell him the same thing, but I can't. My throat gets clogged with insults and nasty things to throw in his face for lying to me all this time.

"Avery, it's okay that you're mad. I don't expect you to forgive me."

He puts his hand on my shoulder, and I lose it. Sobs bubble up from deep inside me, and I fall apart. Tears roll down my cheeks as I stand there blubbering.

"I can't do this! It was bad enough finding out that asshole Victor Campone is my father, but I have a brother too! And he doesn't want to meet me and see how his little sis has been all these years, no! He wants to put a bullet in my head! And when they can't get at me, they strike at those around me. I shouldn't be here, Marty. You'll end up with your throat cut, and—" The snotty crying has gotten so bad that my speech is no longer intelligible.

Marty steps in and wraps his arms around me. He holds me like that until I glance up and see Sean in the living room. I jump back like we were doing something wrong. I wipe the tears from my face and rush past him. When I get to the bathroom, I turn on the shower and cry, not even feeling the water cascade down my body.

They're risking everything for me, and there's no way to ditch either of them. I could run, sneak away in the middle of the night, but Sean will come looking and Marty will help him. I need to do something drastic, something that will make Sean walk away from me.

As I stand there, finally done crying, the hot water easing my sore body, an idea forms. It's horribly cruel and completely final, but it will get Sean to walk away and not look back.

For a moment, I can understand what it must be like for Sean living with the death of his wife because I feel the same aching guilt about him getting sucked into all of this. The sensation only hardens my resolve. I have to do it, and I know he won't forgive me for it.

Not   ever.

Chapter 8

After being cooped up for three days in Marty's beach house, they finally agree it's safe to venture outside, but only after dark. The sun is setting, and Sean and I stroll down the private beach alone.

I tangle our fingers together and try not to focus on the rapid beating of my heart. I lean against him, enjoying the warm feel of his body against mine and wish it could stay this way forever. I want a life where there is nothing to run from, no one to fear. There's only one way to get it. I have to find my brother. I have to dismantle the remains of Victor's mafia, so there is nothing for Sean to take over.

Scenarios turn over in my mind, each ending with me in a body bag. I should have gone to college for something else. My degree does me no good here. Also, I should have taken a freaking gym class. As it is, my thighs are burning trying to walk in the sand. I didn't think I was out of shape. Maybe I'm just tired. Sean squeezes my hand and glances over at me.

"Penny for your thoughts, Miss Smith?" The corners of my lips tug into a small smile.

"You're richer than God and you offer me a penny? Are you cheap, Mr. Jones?"

"Only when it comes to you." He says it deadpan and then smirks.

I stop walking, my jaw dragging on the sand. "You did not just say that!"

"What are you going to do about it?" Sean turns toward me and pulls me to him. He places a hand on my cheek and sweeps his fingers across my skin, leaving a tingly sensation every place he touches.

Reaching up, I put my arms around his neck and pull him toward me, so we're eye to eye.

"Mr. Jones, do you seriously want to be beat up by a girl, right here on the beach? Don't tempt me." There's a smile in my voice even though I'm dying inside.

"Then stop being so damned sexy." He presses the tip of his finger to my nose. "Boop."

I laugh. I can't help it. "Really? 'Boop'?" He nods.

"It's a trick I learned from this hot chick. She's going to be a shrink, so she knows all this Freudian stuff about reading people and getting into their heads. The thing is, she's so far into mine, that I'll never be the same. She has no idea how amazing she is, and how much she's worth. She also thinks she can take on the world alone, but she doesn't have to." His voice is so soft that I can barely hear him over the sound of the waves. We stand there like that, watching each other. "Don't do whatever you're considering doing."

I don't want to deceive him. I don't want things to be like this, but I'm the one pulling him down. I nod and slip my hands down his firm sides, feeling the pads of my fingers slip over each firm muscle until I rest my hands at his waist.

The thought is in my eyes, and I know he sees it. Sean can see right through me, that's why it kills me to say this, but I have to do it. A knife to the heart will add blood to the water. It will taint everything, every emotion, every thought.

Pressing my lips together, I look down at the sand and spit it out. "Sean, I don't want to talk about it now. Talking about this will only make what's already hard, harder." He swallows hard and watches my face.

"That's why you need to tell me. Let me help you." My lips part. I have the words, but swallow them back.

"I'll figure it out. It's not a good time."

"Avery, there's never a good time. Just tell me." He takes my hands, and we stop walking. I'm looking at the sand, trying to find the guts I need to say the words. They're going to rip him in half.

"I think you're right, about Trystan."

He looks surprised, which is good. It means he won't see it coming. It means I was right about this wound still being open. Sean thinks I belong with Trystan.

"I'm surprised to hear you admit it."

I kick the sand and take a step back. I look up at him, careful to meet and hold his gaze. It can't look like I'm lying.

"I knew; I always knew how I felt about him. The thing is, I wanted you more. But Sean, I can't live like this. Terror follows you around. I was yanking your mother's severed arm a few days ago." Tears start to roll down my cheeks.

"Avery, I know, it's hard." He looks scared now.

"Sean, as much as I love you, this isn't going to work." The words slice through me, tearing out my heart as I say them. My tone is level and cool. I sound detached and sincere at the same time.

Sean looks as if I struck him. He blinks once, shocked, and nods. I know he won't refute a plan he created, not when it compromises my safety. I know why Sean wants us together—he thinks I'm in love with Trystan. The insecurity is the size of a grain of sand, but my words make it a mountain. The last part is the worst. For a moment I think I won't be able to do it, but before I can't back down, I say it.

"The thing is, it's not just about me anymore and soon I won't be able to hide it. Do you remember the night Trystan and I disappeared together? Something happened. You were right Sean—there is something between me and Trystan."

Sean is silent. His face is blank, expressionless as I shove the lance through his heart. My stomach twists in knots and I want to cry, but I don't. I can't. He has to believe my story, all of it. Sean's hands drop from my waist. He looks at the surf and asks, "You slept with him?"

"I did." Sean won't detect the lie because I don't know if I'm not telling the truth, for any of it. "There's something else."

Sean turns back to face me, his eyes glassy from tears that refuse to fall. He thinks he was right, that Trystan stole me from him. The lump in my throat is getting too big to speak. I have to tell him the rest. I have to put the final nail in his heart, so he will let me walk away.

"I don't know how to say it, so I'm just going to tell you. We didn't mean for it to happen." I start twisting my hands as I speak and look at the waves crashing on the sand. "It just did. We were both upset and found comfort in each other. That's the thing, Sean—when things with you are bad, Trystan is always there. He's sweet, and he cares about me. That's the only reason I'm not flipping out right now." The wind whips my hair into my face, and it catches in the streams of tears still pouring from my eyes.

"Sean, I'm pregnant. I'm sorry. I'm sorry it's not yours. I can't—"

"Who?"

My jaw drops and I suddenly can't do it. This will kill him. What's left of his soul will shrivel up and die. I reach for him, but Sean pulls away. "Sean, I didn't think we even—"

"A name. You owe me a name." He stands there in the sand with the wind catching his hair and blowing it back into those deep blue eyes. They were once as still as the ocean, and their depths held secrets laced with too much pain for one person to bear. It's too late to undo this, and it's still the best way to keep him safe. Sean would die for me, I know he would—that's why I have to finish. Swallowing hard, I whisper the name.

"Trystan."

The man in front of me turns to stone. Those dark eyes don't blink. They remain fixed on a spot on the shore, as he stands there perfectly still. It's like I sucker-punched him with a mace at the worst time, in the worst way. No matter what Sean wants, there's no future for us. No white picket fences, no little house. Nothing. All these things are racing through his mind. Each thought severs the connection we've found and decimates any hope things will end well for us.

That was the problem—there is no happy ending for us—not with the way things have unraveled. All this time I was the target, not Sean. All this time they were hunting me, and perhaps it wasn't vicious initially, but it is now. There's no way out for me, but if I can get Sean to walk away, he'll live. He'll heal. He can't move forward with me.

My future will end with a toe tag and a body bag.

My stomach churns like I ate glass. I want to puke all over the sand and fall on my face, crying. Everything I did was in vain. Everyone who tried to protect me died. The people around me were deprived of a long life because fate had me cross their paths.

My parents… I can't even think about it. My mother spent her entire life hiding me, my father protected both of us, and in a snap—gone. They died because of me.

My biological father is a murderer who wanted me dead. Since Bryan shot him, I'll never know why. What did I do that warranted a bullet in the head? Was it a vendetta against my mother or me? Marty said I was supposed to die that night, too.

My brother will finish what our father started. If he was willing to go after the Ferro family—if Vic took out Constance—I'm toast. There's no chance I'll walk away from this. I can't condemn Sean to die. I can't pull him down with me.

I feel cruel. I know how this will rip Sean apart. I know what my words are doing to Sean as we stand there in silence. There's no coming back from this point. I walked our relationship to the edge of a cliff and shoved it off.

He wants to walk away. He has to.

Sean stands there, silent for way too long. His face is slack as he stares at the ocean. Memories of us come flooding back. The way he sat with me on the sand, the day he held me and loved me, the fights that always seemed to reconcile—all those memories tainted now. I poisoned the well.

Finally, I walk over and stand next to him. I need to finish. I need to make sure he doesn't pull a Lazarus and come back for me again.

My mouth feels dry and my heart races as I form sentences in my mind, lacing together things I don't want to say.

"Sean, I didn't know how to tell you. I'm sorry."

When he finally speaks, his voice is flat. There's no fight left in him. Sean stares past me, and the only indication that he's upset is the way his jaw tenses.

"We talked about our pasts and lovers— Avery, you lied to me. How could you tell me…" his voice cracks before he can finish. He clears his throat and runs his hands through his hair, pushing it back from his face. When Sean looks up, the sheen in his eyes is gone. The tears that would have fallen will never be shed. He's hardened himself.

I can see him shut me out in those seconds, and it's like having a guillotine drop on my heart.

My tears are real, so real that they burn my skin. They might as well be acid for how much they hurt. I swallow hard and turn to face the wind. It bites at my face and whips my hair. The tightness in my chest is paralyzing, but there was no other way.

Sean will never forgive me for this.

I've destroyed any chance of a future we could have had, but I know Sean will be safe. That's worth it. He'll walk away from all of this. He'll live. Sean will go back to his life in California and make another billion bucks. He'll look back at this time with me as a plague that tormented him. He'll never be the same, but at least he'll live, which is more than I can say about me.

There's still no way for me to get out of this mess without a body bag.

Chapter 9

Sean doesn't speak to me after that. We walk on in silence, and I'm the only one who has wet cheeks. The tears keep falling even though I wish they wouldn't. A fake pregnancy and pretend engagement lie ahead of me. I'll jump through the hoops and hope that I can figure something out so I can find my brother before Trystan gets hurt. I can't let anything happen to him either. He's been through enough.

"You're thinking about him." Sean's voice pulls me from my thoughts and the guilty look on my face is the only answer he needs. "You should have told me. I thought he was attracted to you—I know he is—I just didn't realize it went both ways."

Lie. Avery, you can't tell him it was an accident. You can't tell him you aren't sure what happened that night, the little voice in my head wails. This is torture. I walk faster, pressing my feet against the sand harder and lengthening my stride.

"It does. When you noticed, I felt bad, so I denied it—but we'd already slept together by then." My jaw tightens as I spit out the words.

"So I was right, and Trystan meant it when he said he'd steal you from me. I'm sorry."

"What?" I nearly trip over my feet. Sean catches me by the elbow and turns me toward him. "Why would you say that? You have nothing to be sorry about. I was the one who—" Sean places a finger over my lips as he stares into my eyes.

"I did this. I broke you, neglected you, and pushed you to your limits. When you needed me the most, I threw you together with Trystan. He loves you, Avery. I know you'll be happy together. He can give you everything I can't." Sean's hands linger on my face. He trails his finger along my cheek and pushes a strand of hair behind my ear. I pull away from him, horrified.

"I cheated on you. You didn't make me do it, and I sure as hell didn't slip and fall on his dick! Sean, take this for what it is—the end."

A couple of old people turn toward me while I yell. The old woman has on a sunhat and her lips twitch when I swear. Her eyes are gray, and her skin is wrinkled with age. She leans into her man-friend and whispers something. A moment later, she walks up to Sean, leans in and whispers something. I can't hear a word. Sean looks at her as if she said something absurd. The old woman waggles her pointer finger at him as she walks away.

"Don't forget what I said," she calls with a wink as she turns back to the older man and takes his hand.

That could have been us—old and happy. It's a future we'll never have. I shake the thought from my mind as curiosity takes hold.

"What'd she say?"

"Gibberish, nothing more," Sean says, shaking his head.

I go to grab his arm and stop myself. Sean looks at his arm, at the place I want to touch him. His dark eyes lift and meet mine.

"Sean, won't you tell me?" It feels petty. I just ripped apart his soul, and I'm asking to know what a stranger said in passing. The truth is, he doesn't have to tell me anything anymore. That's what I want, right? To push him away? To keep him safe?

I stop pressing him and lower my gaze. Things have to change. The arrangement is no longer the same. There will never be a ring or a wedding, not with Sean Ferro. The shared secrets will fade like a snowflake on the pad of my finger. I'll remember how he felt, and the shape of his face, but soon those memories will fade, too.

I have no right to ask anything anymore. The thought leaves a path of loneliness in its wake. I wrap my arms around my middle and take a deep breath. Glancing up at him, I force a smile.

"Sorry." It's such a small word, but it means so much.

I'm sorry things ended this way.

I'm sorry I brought so much pain into your life.

I'm sorry death is following me and casting its shadow over you.

I'm sorry things can't be the way we want.

I'm sorry I can't find another way to leave you behind.

I'm sorry I hurt you.

I'm so, so sorry.

He watches me for a moment, his blue eyes slowly searching my face before meeting my gaze. The look lingers, and every regret I have about us plays across his face. It's like he knows how I feel and how much I wish this didn't have to happen.

He thinks the baby is real. It's not.

In that moment, the world fades away. The only thing I can think about is the life I've thrown away. Not the picket fence or the little house, but the real life we could have had together, the real baby that looks like Sean. I mourn the real life of passionate kisses from a man who adores me and midnight conversations that last until dawn.

For the longest time, I only saw the outside of things—the house, the yard, the flowers—not the family within the house. I never realized how much I wanted to hold his child in my arms. Now I never will. I feel like I'm going to be sick, and try to hide it. Sean notices.

"You've been doing all this pregnant. I didn't even notice. I'm sorry for everything, Avery."

He takes a deep breath and looks down the beach at the elderly couple. When he glances back at me, the softness in his gaze fades as his walls go back up.

"She said you're going to have a baby girl. Old people can spot a pregnant woman a mile away. She thought I was the father. I didn't correct her. Come on, let's find Trystan."

Chapter 10

Even though it's night, and there is very little light, I still feel like I'm going to get my head blown off. Their goal is for me to leave and get away with my rock star boyfriend, while the two of them figure out how to get out of this clusterfuck of a mess.

As we approach the shore, there's a little white boat sitting on the sand, two oars stretched across the seat.

"Get in." I climb into the little watercraft and go to sit on the seat while Sean grabs the oars. He shakes his head and points to the spot in front of the bench. "You can't sit up. This plan only works if no one sees you."

Mucky water, sand, and something slimy covers the bottom of the boat. I make a face and nearly protest, but when I look up at Sean, I just do it. I press my body down into the bottom of the boat, resting on something cold and slimy, unable to smell anything but rotting wood.

Sean takes us through the reeds around back, moving the boat insanely slow as to not make a sound. He's constantly looking around, scanning everywhere without moving his head. I can't imagine what's going on inside his beautiful mind. He must feel so betrayed, but I had to do it. Sean isn't indestructible. His mother was indestructible, and still she's dead.

When we pull up to the dock on the opposite shore, I sit up and wipe the slime off my face. Sean grabs a rope and ties it to the boat, then turns to help me onto the dock. We're at a launch a few houses down, directly across from the main road out of here.

"Why'd we come over here?" I don't understand what they're doing. No matter what, I'll be seen going down this road.

"Masterson is meeting us here with a speed boat. He'll drive you to a different port and Trystan will pick you up there. I couldn't risk you being seen leaving from here."

Before I can respond, the hairs on the back of my neck rise. A moment later, the hairs on my arms follow suit, and goose bumps cover my body.

"It feels like someone is watching," I whisper to Sean.

"I know."

"Who is it?" I stumble out of the boat like a drunk ballerina, swirling around to catch my balance. Sean takes my hand and steadies me.

"I don't know, but they had plenty of opportunities to take us out and they haven't."

"So it's a friend?"

His brows crinkle together as if I should already know the answer to that question. He releases my hand and looks over my shoulder before returning his gaze to mine.

"Do you know anyone who would risk their life for you that isn't already here?"

I swallow the sob that wants to come up and shake my head. He hates me. Oh, God!

Sean tips his head to the side, indicating that I should follow him. I try to walk next to him, but Sean doesn't wait for me. His stride is too long, so he's about half a step ahead.

"Trystan isn't that stupid. His distance keeps you alive, so it's not him. Everyone else associated with you seems to have fled. I'm assuming you noticed that, right? Black is silent, Gabe is gone, and Mel ran."

"Mel didn't run. Someone framed her. The cops are still looking for—"

He rounds on me, cutting me off.

"No one is looking for her, Avery! Mel isn't your fucking friend and at the rate you're going, you're going to be lucky if you weren't her mark, too," he yells in a hushed whisper.

"Mark for what? For a fabulous life of hookerdom? What the hell are you talking about?"

He closes his eyes and presses his fingers to his temple. When he looks at me again, he's beyond livid.

"Victor. All this goes back to him. It started with him, and it should have ended with him when Bryan put a bullet in his head, but his shit-for-brains kid showed up. Think about it Avery, why would Victor name you in the will? Why would he insist on dividing his assets between his two kids?"

I look away. I've stopped walking. Wrapping my arms tightly around my middle I stare into space, blinking back tears that can't form.

"I'd rather not think about that man. I have trouble believing he's my biological father, but…" my voice trails off. The way my mother acted all those years, always worried, always looking over her shoulder, it makes more sense now. I suck in air and look at Sean, who has stopped a few steps in front of me. "I know Victor wanted me dead."

"Right, so why put you in his will? It's either to piss off Vic junior or—"

"Or what?"

Sean looks down at me and lowers his lashes. His jaw tightens, and he looks away.

"Or what?" I march over to him, wanting a fight. "Tell me." When he doesn't answer, I shove him and yell, "TELL ME!"

Sean grabs me around my waist and pulls my back to his front in one swift move, before knocking my legs out from under me. We fall to the sand, me face first, with Sean's hand over my mouth to muffle my cries. His body is pressed against me, pinning me to the sand. He twists my head to the side so I can breathe and whispers in my ear.

"It was a final safety precaution. If you lived and Victor died, you would forever be branded as the bastard daughter even Victor Campone didn't want. He branded you. It was a giant, personal fuck you from the afterlife."

The words rip through me, tearing me in two. I fight to get Sean off of me, kicking and twisting until I manage to face him.

"That was the nastiest thing you've ever said to me."

"It's true. The man hated your mother and clearly didn't want you. He spent his life trying to erase you." Sean's voice is hard and even. His gaze is closed off, devoid of emotion. I can feel his lungs expand as he breathes in, making his body press against mine. The way he looks at me, the way he's drowning in betrayal and mistrust, makes me die inside. I want to wrap my arms around him and tell him the truth, but I can't.

I hate feeling him this close. I hate that his words are true. Now that Sean's said it, there's no erasing the thought.

Sprawling my fingers, I grab a fistful of sand and throw it at his face. The wind catches it and blows most of it the wrong way. As soon as my fist opens, Sean grabs my wrist and pins it down. He uses the rest of his body to hold me in place so I can't move.

"The truth is, we're both fucked up people no one wanted. Learn to live with it." Sean releases me and pushes up. He's on his feet and walking toward the house again without a backward glance.

I deserved that, I know I did, but he hurt me with the one wound that would bleed forever.

I guess that makes us even.

Chapter 11

I follow Sean down the shoreline, walking in the loose sand up by the dunes, for a mile or more. My muscles are burning. Every step I take feels like someone is jamming knives in my thighs. Sean is ahead of me, walking fast, not bothering to turn around. His t-shirt was white, but it's now clinging to his sweat-covered body. His jeans ride low around his trim waist, and it's hard not to notice how beautiful he is.

I swallow hard and force my gaze to the sand. I can't think of him like that anymore. I need to figure out how to find my deranged brother and end this. I've got to get both of them to walk away from me first. I think Sean is ready to do that. A few more nasty words and he's gone.

An idea forms and I decide to follow it through. Chasing after Sean, I rush up beside him. "Ferro, wait up!"

Sean doesn't look at me or slow his stride. His legs are pure muscle. The man is a god, showing no sign of strain other than his glistening body.

"Hey!" I grab his arm and tug. "I'm talking to you! Stop!" Sean jerks his arm away.

"We don't have time to chat, Avery. Vic is looking for us, Marty is risking his life, and someone is following us. Whatever you want to say doesn't matter. Keep walking." Sean's brow pinches together when he turns away and starts to take a step. I round in front of him and hold up two hands. He plows right into me.

"Holy shit, Sean!" I nearly fall over. Sean doesn't try to steady me. Instead, he tries to keep walking. I yell out as he passes, "I wanted to tell you something, but if you're going to be such an asshole, you don't deserve it."

He stops. His body tenses, shoulder blades nearly touching, and he rounds on me, getting up in my face.

"I don't deserve it? I'm the one who was unfaithful and got knocked up? Oh, wait, that was you!" His eyes narrow into thin slits, and the way he looks at me makes me worry. The old Sean is still there, waiting to consume him. I don't know how far I can push without destroying him. The wind whips my hair into my face. I shove it back and launch into it.

"You put me with him! I wanted you, but where were you, Sean? Gone! You weren't there when I needed someone the most! You're never there!"

Tears fall from my eyes. I'm using his insecurities against him, driving the wedge between us so hard we'll crack apart and never recover. There won't be anything left after this. He'll walk away from me.

"I was taking care of people I love. Some of them have gotten into deep shit, and you know what? No one else helped, but I could, so I did. I'm sorry I couldn't hold your hand and coddle you. I'm sorry I made you hang out with a rock star and dress like a slut on stage and dance with him. If I'd never done that, I wouldn't have lost you."

As he speaks, the bluster in his tone dies down, and his gaze softens. No! He can't forgive me. What the hell is he doing? He was supposed to fight back, but he's backing down. I shove his chest hard, and he steps back. I do it again, slapping hard.

"That's not good enough! You were never around! You put everyone else before me, even your mother! She didn't even love you! You ran into a fucking war zone for someone who hates you!"

Sean remains utterly still. His chest doesn't rise or fall. His eyes don't blink. His lips are the only thing that move, and as I speak, they part and his jaw drops lower and lower. Every shot is below the belt, precisely aimed to eliminate any fondness he still felt toward me. I prey on his weaknesses and vulnerabilities. The Sean I love, the open version of him that was so hard to draw out, will never appear again.

I lock my jaw in place and tense the muscles to prevent their quivering. I'm ready to cry, but I can't. He'll know what I'm doing if I suddenly break down weeping.

Finish this.

Mashing my lips together, I cast the final stone, the one that will shatter everything.

"I never loved you. How could I? You're a monster, Sean Ferro. You were my mark from day one. Miss Black wanted you on her client list, and I told her I'd get you to sign." As I speak, the muscles in Sean's arms cord tightly until the vein in his neck jumps up. It's pulsing hard, anger flooding his body. His hands flex into fists. I keep talking, spewing lies until he cracks. "It was never about you. I wanted your money, and she wanted her thumb on a Ferro. You were a business acquisition, and nothing more."

He rushes at me, his hands on my shoulders gripping me hard. His blue eyes are somewhere between livid and wounded. His voice is barely audible.

"You don't mean that. None of that is true."

"You're so naïve. You only see what you want to see; you've been played. Your first instinct was correct, Black set you up and you fell for it."

He works his jaw for a moment and then asks, "How could you do this to me?" His eyes meet mine, holding my gaze, waiting for the answer that will destroy him. My words will send him straight back to the hell he resided in for so long. My lips part and I know what I need to say, but the words won't come. I start to tremble and then manage to twist away from him, pulling out of his grip. I step back once, and then again. I'm standing between the grass plants on the dunes. Looking at the sand, I spit it out. I have to. He has to walk away, or he'll die. My lips quiver slightly, but my voice is firm and flat.

"You murdered your wife and unborn child. Do you really think I'd have any empathy for a wife killer? Who needs family planning when you're around?"

I look up as I say the last part. I have to make sure he believes me. I watch those blue eyes fill with anguish as I speak. For a moment, he says nothing. Then Sean falls forward, face-first into the sand. My eyes widen when I see a man standing behind him with a gun in hand. I glance back down at Sean to see red blossoming from a single point on the back of his shirt.

The man is thin with dark hair peeking from a once-shaved scalp. A tattoo wraps around the back of his skull. I can't tell what it is from here. Every muscle is showing through his tanned skin, corded tight, like rope. He tips his head to the side, and four other guys—huge scary looking men—immediately flank him.

"Take out the trash."

He stares at Sean as his men grab him by his arms and drag him to the water. Sean is still alive, swearing, trying to pull away, but he can't. One man holds him while the other thrusts his face into the water and holds him there. Sean's arms and legs flail as they try to drown him.

I rush forward, ready to beg for Sean's life, but the man applauds slowly, one clap at a time.

"That was fucking beautiful. You played this asshole for months, strung him along, and led him straight to me. No wonder why Pop didn't want you around. You're one heartless bitch." He follows my gaze to the water where I'm watching Sean struggle less and less. Vic snaps his fingers, and his thugs pull Sean's face out of the water.

Sean comes up gasping and choking. His entire shirt is bright red and clinging to his back. Sand sticks to the side of his face as water rolls down his cheeks. He looks up and sees me standing next to my brother. The way his eyes flash with understanding scares the hell out of me.

Sean's voice is rough. He spits onto the sand and tries to pull away from the men holding him, but he's too weak. He glares at me.

"You fucking whore. It was you." He chokes again and lifts his sagging body, before trying to rush at me. Vic's men hold him back. "It was you! This whole time, everything that happened, everyone who died! It's your fucking fault! You were working together from the beginning!"

It feels like he stabbed me in the stomach with an icicle. Fear races through my veins as he pieces everything together, forming a pattern that lines up with my other lies. He thinks I planned this together—that Vic and I were coming at his family from different sides. Without the Ferro clan in the way, my family keeps a firm control on New York—on every wealthy family, every corrupt businessman, and every two-faced politician.

I'm so dead. We both are if I don't say the right thing right now.

I glance over at my brother and step closer to him with a soft, confident smile on my face.

"Blood is thicker than water. You better remember that next time I see you. Oh, wait. There won't be a next time." I arch a single brow at him, feigning confidence and turn on my heel.

Vic laughs and snaps his fingers again.

"Get rid of him."

The men drag Sean away, even though he fights to break free. I hope they can hold him because if they can't, I'm dead. He won't wait for me to say a word, not with the nails I drove into his heart over the past few days. I finally had my beautiful, caring, vulnerable Sean, and I destroyed him.

SHADOWS OF THE PAST

by

H.M. WARD
&
Stacey Mosteller

A free excerpt from the newest stand alone novel by H.M. Ward & Stacey Mosteller.

Turn the page to read more!

PREFACE

Coming to Europe should have changed things, but I was wrong. It didn't ease the pain, and the distance only makes me feel alone. The woman I was four years ago doesn't exist anymore. In her place, an empty shell of who I was fakes her way through the motions of living life. Inside, I stay closed off, terrified of opening up to more pain and loss. The shadows of the past drag me under, keeping me constantly gasping for relief.

This time of year, and everything it represents, is horrible. Today is the anniversary of the day my life changed forever—again. Instead of celebrating fourth birthdays and putting ribbons in their hair, blowing out candles, and listening to their laughter, I'm stuck in an endless loop of nothing.

The alarm clock buzzes again. I smack it with my pillow and knock it on the floor where it continues to buzz. Damn. I pivot in the bed and reach down, extending my arm as far as possible. I manage to whack the button, which quickly turns it off. Once again, I'm shrouded in the silence.

After four years as a nomad, I want to forget for just a second. For those first few minutes of each day, it's as if I'm waking from a bad dream. I close my eyes and see their sweet faces, smiling. Then reality sets in and my soul feels ripped apart with grief. The weight at the center of my chest crushes me, making me fight for air.

Images, memories pour into my mind in an unrelenting wave. One thought after another. I relive the nightmare, seeing it behind my eyes every time I blink. Tears streak down my face soaking my pillow. I'm fully awake and…

I remember.

CHAPTER 1

"This is stupid," I blurt out as I tug the hemline of my way too short dress down. Emily swats at me.

"No, it's not. You seem out of it lately, and there's no bloody way I'm letting you sit at home and swallow a bottle of booze. You need to choose a different bad habit before you turn into a wine-o."

Emily is a sweet little rich girl. Her daddy bought her a flat in London a few years back, and it's in the perfect location for me—right by Kensington Park. When I first arrived in London a few months ago, I'd wander the park for hours lost in thought.

Then I met Emily.

Now I'm wearing a slutty dress with fuck-me heels. Emily practically yanked my sweatpants off to get me to go out. Now I'm all dolled up with a plan, but my stomach is twisting in knots.

I stop abruptly. "I can't do this."

Emily rounds on me, taking my hands. "Yes, you can. One night will help you feel better, and get rid of that sourpuss." She squeezes my cheeks together and smirks.

I bat her hand away. "I'm not like you. I can't just walk up to a guy and say let's do it."

Emily laughs. "Don't be crass! You don't have to say a thing; that dress says it all for you." She arches a dark brow at me. It stands in contrast to her fair skin and pale hair.

"Compared to you, I look like a tramp."

"You are a tramp—tonight, anyway. Then tomorrow you can go back to be the secretive, sulky flatmate who is going to let me adopt a cat." She waggles her eyebrows at me.

"Again with the cat thing?" I fold my arms over my chest.

Emily gazes down at my neckline and smirks. "Nice cleavage, but I'm already seeing someone." I frown and put my arms down, ready to turn back and bury myself in a mountain of blankets. Crying for hours sounds like a great way to spend the night. Okay, maybe not. I'm tired of crying. I feel so consumed by grief I can't remember who I am anymore.

Emily smiles quickly and takes my hand. She's so touchy-feely. I'm uncomfortable, but I don't jerk away from her because she's just trying to help.

"Listen, I know today means something to you—something bad. Let's go in and find some dashing fellow to help you forget, just for the night. And if we don't find a match who meets your standards, we'll both get smashed and wobble home together."

"Fine, but I don't do girls." I'm teasing. Emily changed teams a while back and has a girlfriend.

She nods. "Yes, I know. You've told me. Frequently. I won't hit on you, even though you look delicious in my dress. The last time I wore that…" she touches her fingers to her red lips and giggles. Glancing at me out of the corner of her eyes, she adds, "Well, let's just say that dress hit the floor fast."

There's a chill in the night air and the familiar sounds of London evenings fill my ears. Inhaling deeply, I fall into step with Emily again, heading for the swanky new pub she's been gushing about for weeks. These heels are much higher than I'm used to, so we walk slowly down the street. At the same time, I'm aware of male eyes sliding over my body in this tight red dress. I'm treated to several smiles and a wink.

As we get to the place, Emily grabs my hand. "Listen, tonight you're someone else—no names, no contact, no commitment. Just fun. Got it?"

My stomach dips, but my resolve solidifies. "Got it. I'm someone else." I can do this. I can jump into bed with a guy and roll around, have fun, and then bolt. I don't need the rest, but something about this prospect makes me feel hollow inside.

I shrug the feeling off and look at Emily. She's waiting for me to decide if I'm going to do it. At that moment, a man walks up behind us, cutting the entire line. His dark hair and toned body make him look like a model. His gaze is on the sidewalk, and his shoulders hunch forward. For a split second, he glances at me. Our eyes lock and hold. I feel pinned in place, breathless. Emily is still talking, but I can't hear her. My world flips to slow motion as I remain locked in a staring contest with this sexy stranger.

The shadows under his eyes make me wonder what hell he's been through. He doesn't look like the kind of man to get lost in liquor. Everything about him is sleek, put together, and proper. I'm sure that's who he is, or who he was before whatever made him upset. From the look in his eyes, the pain is raw—still fresh.

He breaks the gaze and disappears through the door. My heart is pounding in my chest, but I'm not sure why.

Emily glares at me with her huge eyes and rams my shoulder.

"Hello? Earth to Kayla. Are we going in or not?"

Nodding slowly, I step forward and reach for the door. "I'm in. Help me find a hook-up, wingman."

CHAPTER 2

For a city that's older than dirt, what the heck is the attraction to the super modern style? The inside of this place is made entirely of chrome and glass. Silver metal barstools at super sleek, skinny glass tables. There are no linens anywhere, no curtains, nothing soft or warm. The floor is white and pulses under a black light that surrounds the perimeter of the room.

The barstool is a little high for a dress this short and tight. Since the tables are transparent, there's no place to hide. I feel exposed.

Emily turns to me, swirling the remainder of the drink in her cocktail glass.

"I need another. I'll get you a refill too. Be right back." Emily slips off the stool and walks like she's not sloshed, over to the bar.

Music blares as people pack into the crowded space. Pubs and nightclubs seem to be London's only evening entertainment options. Everything else closes after dinner. I wish I were joking. Transitioning from the city that never sleeps to London was strange at first. The long lonely nights sucked. When I first arrived, I got stuck on the other side of town and had to ride back on the night bus. That was scarier than walking through Times Square in the middle of the night when the orange jumpsuits are cleaning up.

God, I was dumb. Speaking of dumb, I should probably call a car to take us home. Just one more drink and neither of us will be able to walk, much less call a taxi without sounding idiotic.

"Hullo." A deep voice comes from behind me.

Based on the other greetings I've gotten tonight, this one is tame. I turn slowly in my seat and look over my shoulder at him. It's the guy from outside. His shoulders are straight, but he still has that kicked puppy look in his eyes.

"Hi," I say shyly, looking up at him from under my lashes.

The guy looks over at the counter and points to my table. "Share a drink with me."

I smirk. "Since you asked so nicely…"

"You don't want nice, not tonight. You want a fling, a meaningless sweaty night with a stranger." The way he says it makes me freeze. "What's the matter, love? Cat got your tongue?"

I shake off my shock. His audacity prompts a slow smile to spread across my lips.

"Great pick up line. Do you use it on all the girls? Or am I special?"

He smirks and slides into Emily's empty chair. Placing one hand on his knee he leans back and surveys me. Pushing his hand through his dark hair, he laughs.

"Tell me, American Girl, why else would you be wearing a dress that hugs that sinful body if you weren't on the prowl this evening? Do you enjoy tormenting the opposite sex? Or are you just afraid of relinquishing control and having a good time?"

My jaw drops and I gasp. "You don't even know me!"

He scans my body with a smug look. Leaning toward me, he whispers, "I know enough. Your thighs are pinned together as if no man could pry them apart."

"Well, you certainly won't." I laugh, pushing my long dark hair over my shoulder. Then I glance around for Emily, but I don't see her.

"No, I won't. I don't dip my wick in crazy." He smirks again, showing off that lopsided, lickable smile.

"Neither do I."

He glances down at my lap and back up to my face. "Really? I wouldn't have taken you for a man at all. Where do you hide your dick in that dress?"

My jaw drops and I gape. Before I realize what I'm doing, I shove his arm.

"That's not what I meant. You're a jerk. Go bother someone else." I stare pointedly ahead but from the corner of my eye, I notice a wicked grin light up his face.

"Am I really bothering you?" I let out an exasperated sigh. "Right, I thought not. Ah, here we are. Just in time." He looks up at a woman carrying a tray. "Place those right here, love. Cheers!"

After she leaves, I arch an eyebrow at him. "So, how'd you get her to bring shots over to the table?"

"Really? That's your question? I thought you'd be more interested in what we're drinking." He gestures toward the golden liquid in the little glasses. The barkeep also brought limes and salt in clear, square bowls.

"I have eyes."

"Yes, you do. They're spectacular if I might say so."

"You may," I say with an indulgent sideways glance at him. I reach forward to grab a lime slice and salt. With my eyes on his, I lick the skin between my thumb and pointer finger before sprinkling it with salt.

He watches me but doesn't take a glass. He doesn't even move.

"What?" I ask, frowning.

"You're very expressive when you're irritated." Leaning in close, like he's going to tell me a secret, "It's sexy."

His warm breath against my skin makes me shiver. When he straightens, his eyes appear to be a darker shade of blue, causing my breath to catch in my throat. Before I can get my equilibrium back, he licks the salt off my hand and downs the shot.

Shocked, I stare at him with my mouth open.

He grins. Reaching forward, he presses his finger under my jaw and lifts. My lips close.

"Gaping isn't as sexy. Well, I guess it depends on what we're doing at the time. Do you find me shocking love? Or do you behave like this around all British men? Is this how you behave in America?"

Inexplicably, my cheeks burn. I press my eyes shut and gather my thoughts. I'm here for a reason. Pull it together, Kayla. This guy wants me; I'm clearly attracted to him, so what's stopping me? Besides my innate need to bicker?

"Dear Lord! You're blushing!" He looks shocked. Before I he says anything else, I act.

Feeling brave, I take his hand in mine, which silences him instantly. He watches as I lift his palm to my lips and lick his skin. His breath catches and his back goes rigid, his deep blue eyes watch me shake salt across his moistened skin. Slowly I slide my tongue over the salt, licking it up. He stops breathing at the first swipe of my tongue across his flesh, then watches me intently as I down the shot before biting into a slice of lime.

"Bloody hell." His voice is raspy, deeper. He shifts in his chair and watches me. The rawness of his pain is still close to the surface. I can see it flicker when I move. It's as if he's trying to shove his past behind him—for just a night— and forget. I know we're on the same page, looking for the same thing. I down my shot, slam my glass down, and lean into his shoulder.

"How crazy are you?" My comment startles him. Proper Dude straightens and looks down at me.

"Well, I can honestly say no woman has asked me that before."

"So, then you're more of the closet crazy type, huh?"

"Come again?" His brow wrinkles.

"Ooh, a dirty talker." I giggle softly and hold onto his arm, testing the waters. He's firm under those fine clothes.

"Hardly," he returns with a smirk. "At least not in establishments such as this. I don't bang women in the loo either."

"Good to know. I've never been fond of bathroom bangers." His muscle firms up as I lean into him, squeezing his arm.

He smiles at me. "Are you serious?" I offer a flippant expression that's noncommittal. The alcohol is spreading through me, and I know the play on words is a bit crass, but I don't care. "I can't tell if you realize what you're saying or not."

"That's for me to know and you to find out." I'm snuggling his arm, when he lifts my chin. In response to his touch, I straighten and let him hold my gaze. I'm no longer fighting the death grip that was holding onto me when we walked in. I could melt into this guy.

"You have no grasp of local euphemisms, do you?"

"Psh," I say, and smile before lifting my hand to his cheek. His face feels warm under my fingers. I want to trace his jaw and feel that stubble glide beneath the pads of my fingers. "I know enough. For example, all men are wankers, but all wankers aren't men."

He laughs. "That settles that debate." He leans in closing the distance between us. The pull inside me is so strong it rips me out of my buzz. I notice how warm I've gotten, and it worries me. I haven't felt this way in a really long time. Sparring helps it seem less real, so I smirk and pull back a little.

"So spill," I say as I scoot back in my chair. Somehow I ended up on the edge, nose to nose with him. If I go home with this guy, I need to know he won't kill me and toss my body in the Thames. Hot guy doesn't let me back away. Instead, he scoots closer to me and takes my hand.

"Ask away."

My stomach flips. Swallowing hard, I ask, "Fetishes, warrants, criminal record? And then tell me what gets your freak on."

The man actually giggles. He tries to pull away, his cheeks flaming with embarrassment, but I lace my hands around his neck and hold him in place.

"I'll go first, "Yes, no, yes—and no freaky fetish stuff."

He arches an eyebrow at me. "Nothing freaky?"

"You would fixate on that part. It's your turn now."

"You're very direct, American Girl."

"I'm a New Yorker."

"I can tell. I feel like you might castrate me if I answer incorrectly."

"There is no wrong answer at this point— only the truth. And don't lie to me, or this is over. I want to know what I'm walking into."

He grins again, his blue eyes darting to the side and back as if he's considering telling me something.

"Fetishes—not tonight. Warrants—none. Criminal record—none. I'm not a colorful person in that regard."

I've been tracing his cheek while we talk. Nothing is setting off my crazy-o-meter, which makes me realize that this is going to happen. I don't have to go home and cry. I won't have to relive this night again. My eyes glass over as the thought flashes and fades.

Hot guy notices. He leans in and takes my face between his palms and rubs his thumb over my cheek.

"I noticed you outside and can tell we're in similar positions this evening. I don't do this—at all—and honestly you're somewhat intimidating, but I feel drawn to you." The confession startles me, as does the affection in his voice.

My chest tightens and I want to wrap my arms around him and hold on tight. He seems like an anchor in a storm, a safe spot. Leaning in slowly, I close the distance between us and brush my lips against his. The result is immediate. Shocks cascade through my body, electrifying my skin and torching my insides. My heart slams into my chest so rapidly I can't breathe.

We both pull back and stare with mirrored expressions of shock and that four-letter dirty word—hope. I see it in his eyes and felt it when we kissed. There was a connection that's deep and pure. It startled both of us, and hardly anything does that anymore.

I sputter out, "This isn't going to happen."

He stares at me, wide-eyed. His lips part, but Emily cuts him off.

She perches on the seat opposite him and reaches out for his tie. Grabbing it, she yanks the guy forward.

"Listen, if you hurt her I will track you down, and feed your balls to my cat—while they're still attached to your body."

I bury my face in my hands. "Emily, stop."

"Good to know." Hot guy pulls his tie back and glances at me. "This one should come with a wick warning."

I laugh. I can't help it. "That's on her other shirt."

Emily frowns. "Fine, go off together and have hot, hairy sex. See if I care."

"Hairy?" We both say in unison and look at Emily, then each other. She leans back in her seat and looks over at the bar.

"If you end up dead under a bridge, it's not my fault. I warned you."

I put my hand to the side of my mouth and say in a loud whisper, "Is she talking to you?"

"I thought she was addressing you. Unless you have something dangly to tell me about, of the hairy variety—"

My jaw drops. "No!"

"Well, you mentioned a wick once already. I wouldn't want to get you home and find that you really DO have one under that dress."

Emily laughs. "Straight people are weird. If you're not into her, I can take her home tonight instead." Emily winks at me.

I want to punch her, but instead I squirm in my seat. To my surprise, hot guy takes my hand, helps me up, and hands me my purse before addressing Emily.

"As much fun as it is chatting with you, Emily, I need to take your friend." He cuts off like he was going to say more, but didn't.

"Uh," I babble, "that meant something else since you didn't finish the sentence."

"I think you caught my meaning."

He looks down at me, intense once again. The sensations shooting through my body originate at the point of contact. His touch is electric and all consuming to the point that I shiver.

"Here, take my coat." Before I can protest, he has it wrapped around my shoulders. Damn, it smells good—like him. He presses his hand to my back and guides us to the door. Emily's laughter rings out from behind me.

"Remember to use protection," she shouts across the pub. A few male voices snigger. Before I fully realize what happened, we're outside.

"Your friend is very, unique."

Rubbing my arms, I look up and down the street. "That's one word for it." Hot Guy turns me toward him.

"I like you. I want to see where this goes. Come with me." His confidence is contagious, and I find myself nodding, even though my mind is screaming for me to run the other way.

A sleek black Bentley pulls up to the curb, interrupting my thoughts. I glance at him. "Who are you?"

"No names tonight, American Girl. We both know that's not what we want."

I press my lips together and look up at him. Hot Guy opens my door and waits. Part of me wants to run—the attraction to this guy is too strong—but the other part of me knows I can't go home. Heart racing, I reach for his outstretched hand and slip into the car.

COMING SOON

THE ARRANGEMENT 20

Don't miss it! Pre-order NOW!

*****

To ensure you don't miss H.M. Ward's next book, text AWESOMEBOOKS (one word) to 22828 and you will get an email reminder on release day.

*****

Want to talk to other fans?
Go to *Facebook* and join the discussion!

MORE FERRO FAMILY BOOKS

NICK FERRO
~THE WEDDING CONTRACT~
*****

BRYAN FERRO
~THE PROPOSITION~
*****

SEAN FERRO
~THE ARRANGEMENT~
******

PETER FERRO GRANZ
~DAMAGED~
******

JONATHAN FERRO
~STRIPPED~
******

**MORE ROMANCE BY
H.M. WARD**

SCANDALOUS

SCANDALOUS 2

SECRETS

THE SECRET LIFE OF TRYSTAN SCOTT

DEMON KISSED

CHRISTMAS KISSES

SECOND CHANCES

And more.

To see a full book list, please visit:
www.sexyawesomebooks.com/#!/BOOKS

CAN'T WAIT FOR H.M. WARD'S NEXT STEAMY BOOK?

Let her know by leaving stars and telling her
what you liked about
THE ARRANGEMENT 19
in a review!

COVER REVEAL:

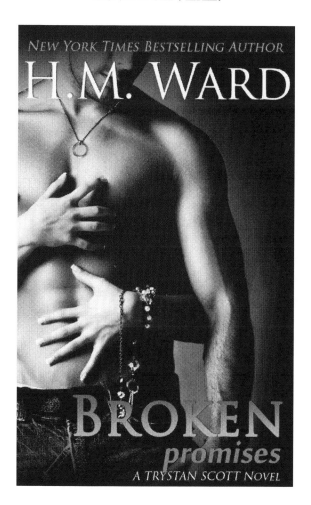